SERVICE LEARNING

Volunteering to Help Kids

Michael A. Black

HIGH
interest
books

Children's Press
A Division of Grolier Publishing
New York / London / Hong Kong / Sydney
Danbury, Connecticut

Photo Credits: Cover, p. 7, 11, 12, 15, 17, 18, 26, 29, 30, 33, 34
© Indexstock; p. 4, 38, 41 © Corbis; p. 8, 21, 22, 36 © Skjold

Contributing Editors: Mark Beyer and Rob Kirkpatrick
Book Design: Michael DeLisio

Visit Children's Press on the Internet at:
http://publishing.grolier.com

Library of Congress Cataloging-in-Publication Data

Black, Michael A.
    Volunteering to help kids / by Michael A. Black.
        p. cm. – (Service learning)
    Includes bibliographical references and index.
    Summary: Gives examples of different service-learning programs that ben-
    efit children and gives advice about starting new programs.
    ISBN 0-516-23372-6 (lib. bdg.) – ISBN 0-516-23572-9 (pbk.)
    1. Student service—Juvenile literature. 2. Voluntarism—Juvenile literature.
    [1. Student service. 2. Voluntarism.] I. Title. II. Series.

LC220.5.B56 2000
362.71—dc21

                                                        00-026677

CONTENTS

INTRODUCTION

In 1960, President John F. Kennedy talked about the importance of volunteering to help others. "Ask not what your country can do for you—ask what you can do for your country," he said. He took that message to the nation's youth. Many young people joined volunteer organizations such as VISTA (Volunteers In Service To America) and the Peace Corps. They met new people and experienced many different things. They became better citizens and stronger individuals.

One of these young men later became president himself. His name is Bill Clinton. In 1993, President Clinton signed the National

President John F. Kennedy shakes hands with Sargent Shriver, the first director of the Peace Corps.

and Community Service Trust Act. This started new service-learning programs all over the nation.

These nationwide organizations are not the only type of service-learning programs. Many schools around the country offer their own service-learning programs. Some motivated students even start their own projects, with the help of teachers or parents. For thousands of young people throughout the United States and Canada, service learning provides a great opportunity for helping the community and helping yourself at the same time.

You should meet with a teacher or counselor when you plan your project.

CHAPTER ONE

WHAT IS SERVICE LEARNING?

Service-learning and community-service programs use volunteer (unpaid) workers to help in the community. However, service learning goes one step further. Service-learning volunteers work on learning about themselves. The philosophy of service learning is that, through helping people in your community, you develop new skills and learn more about your interests and abilities.

HELPING KIDS IN THE COMMUNITY

In every town, village, and city, there are children who need help. Some need help learning how to read or play sports. Some need

Service learners can help children get safely across the street.

9

help finding their way around a new school. Some need safe places to play on weekends. Some need places to go after school. Some even need donations of food and clothing. Service-learning volunteers have many opportunities to help kids in the community.

HELPING OTHERS HELPS YOU

Service-learning is not just about helping other people. You can learn new skills in a service-learning program. By helping to organize people, you gain management skills. By writing and talking to community officials, you gain communication skills. By seeing a project through to its completion, you develop discipline. The benefits go both ways.

School Credit

Some schools give academic credit to students who participate in service-learning programs. Ask your guidance counselor if your school has such a program. You may be

Ask your guidance counselor about service learning.

required to keep a journal or make a presentation about your service-learning experiences.

College Application

The skills you develop during a service-learning program will help you later in life. If you plan to go to college, your volunteer work may help you get into the college of your

*Job interviewers may enjoy hearing about
your service-learning experience.*

choice. A college application will have a section
where you can list and describe your volunteer
activities. College admissions departments like
to accept candidates who have this kind of
extracurricular (outside of class) experience.

Resumé

You can benefit from your service-learning
work when it comes time for you to get a job.

When you apply for a job, you will need to give the employer a list of your past experiences. This list is called a resumé. Service-learning experience looks great on a resumé.

Ready for the Real World

Your service-learning experience will help you when you are done with school, too. You will learn how to solve problems, organize events, budget your time, and work with others. These skills will prove valuable in any field of work.

A PRESIDENTIAL THANK-YOU

To further help the service-learning programs across the country, there is the President's Student Learning Challenge. Each high school in the country may choose one junior or senior service-learner to get a one thousand-dollar scholarship. Scholarship winners receive a gold pin, a certificate, and a letter from the president. To be considered for the scholarship, service-learners must have served at least one hundred hours in a twelve-month period.

PROGRAMS THAT HAVE HELPED KIDS

There are service-learning programs already out there that have helped kids in different towns and cities. The volunteers in these programs provide a good model for others wishing to volunteer their time and effort.

Teen Helpers

More than two hundred teens from fifteen schools across the country participate in the Early Adolescent Helper Program. These schools are located in such cities as New York City; Bridgeport, Connecticut; and Phoenix, Arizona. The students volunteer to help with day care, child after-school care programs, and sport activities. They do a variety of different things to help people. They tell stories to children. They take younger kids on trips to

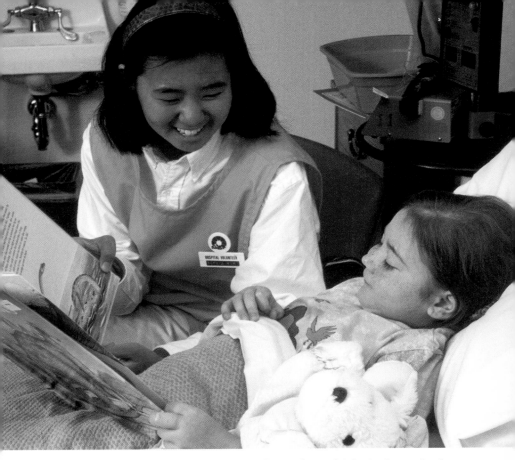

Service learners can become friends to kids in hospitals.

parks and museums. Each Early Adolescent Helper group meets once a week with a teacher or adult leader to discuss its activities.

Volunteers in Mount Vernon
In 1987, a school district in Mount Vernon, Washington, started its own service-learning

program. All students participated in some way. Fourth graders helped teach first graders how to read. Second graders helped clean the school. High school students taught Spanish to kids in second and third grade.

Aid to Autistic Children

Some children are born with a mental disorder that prevents them from talking or playing with other children. The disorder makes them shut out the rest of the world. This condition is called autism.

An Illinois high school service-learning program called the Leo Group works with autistic children. Volunteers teach autistic kids how to do such things as walk around the classroom, and how to go up and down stairs. The Leo Club has more than two hundred volunteer members. It is one of the largest service-learning groups in the nation.

Service learners can work on projects that help children with special challenges.

CHAPTER TWO

JOINING A SERVICE-LEARNING PROGRAM

So you're looking to get into service learning but don't know where to begin? First, you need to find a school or organization that sponsors a service-learning program. Second, you need to find an activity in this program that interests you. Then, decide whether you will have the time and commitment necessary to join.

STARTING IN YOUR SCHOOL

Most schools have clubs and teachers that can direct you. With their guidance, pick a volunteer activity that you will enjoy. If you enjoy reading, you can read to younger

Teachers can help by offering their experience and knowledge.

children or even help them learn how to read. If you are good at baseball, you can coach beginning players on how to swing a bat or use a glove. Do you play a musical instrument? It's always fun to share your music with others. You can help a class of younger students put on their own play. You can even help a teacher lead a field trip to the zoo. Talk to your teacher or guidance counselor and see what kind of opportunities are at your school.

Taking ACT-ion

Social studies teachers across the country have a program available called ACT (Active Citizenship Today). This program is sponsored by the Close Up Foundation and the Constitutional Rights Foundation. Students are asked to pick a topic and then create a program to teach younger kids. The service-learners teach kids about such topics as crime, violence, and drug abuse.

AmeriCorps volunteers teach kids to read.

PUBLIC AND PRIVATE SPONSORS

Schools are not the only places where you can find a service-learning program to join. Organizations in both the public sector (government) and private sector (business and industry) fund programs that help kids.

Public Programs

In 1993, President Bill Clinton formed AmeriCorps to act as a domestic Peace Corps. AmeriCorps has provided a number of rewarding experiences to young volunteers.

AmeriCorps volunteeers use their experience in tutoring.

In 1997, a Utah student used her AmeriCorps experience to help her start a tutoring program for a local elementary school. She also organized local residents and college students to rescue a nearby lot that had become a drug-dealing area.

In 1995, an AmeriCorps volunteer in Colorado developed a smoke-free campaign for local schools. One year before, an AmeriCorps leader in Idaho helped to start a program for giving immunization shots to toddlers. The number of Idaho children who got shots went way up. The volunteer later pursued a career in health care.

Private Programs

Not all service-learning programs are government-funded. There are a number of service organizations run by private businesses and charities. The Challenge Learning Center (CLC) is an example of one such program. At the CLC, volunteers learn how to lead outdoor programs for disadvantaged children. After their CLC training, service workers are able to teach children about the outdoors through wilderness hikes and rock climbing in the American West. A key part of the CLC program is learning how to work together with others. Its volunteers often use the phrase, "There is no failure, only feedback."

SELECTING A PROJECT

Are you ready to join a service-learning organization? Great! Wanting to volunteer your time is the first step. Then you need to figure out what kind of program you want to join!

Interests

What do you like to do? Do you like to read? Are you good at sports? Do you enjoy meeting new people? Whatever you like to do, the best volunteer is one who performs tasks that he or she enjoys.

FAST FACT

Almost 5.5 million middle school and high school students are doing service learning.

Abilities

What skills can you offer to a service-learning group? Are you a good letter writer? Do you know a lot about nature and the outdoors? Are you good at organizing people? If you can identify any special skills you have, you will be able to describe them to a service-learning leader.

Goals

Why do you want to join service learning? Are you looking to gain work experience? Do you need school credit? Are you looking to help yourself feel better? The answers to these questions will help you to identify the type of project you want to join.

COMMITMENT

Before joining a service-learning project, you must figure out how much time you can volunteer. What is your schedule like? Can you volunteer your time after school? Can you work on the weekends? Once you join a project, your service-learning leader will depend on you for a certain time commitment. Be realistic in saying how much time you have to give. The best service learners know how much they can give and then use that time to help the group.

CHAPTER THREE

STARTING A PROJECT TO HELP KIDS

Maybe your school or community does not offer a service-learning program that interests you. Or maybe you have volunteered in one of these programs but want to form your own. It will take a lot of work, but you can do it.

SETTING A GOAL

First, you have to decide what kind of project you want to do. Once you've decided what it is you want to do, set a goal. Keep it simple, especially if this is your first service-learning project. Nothing is more frustrating than trying to do too many things. A small project with a solid goal can do a lot of good.

At the beginning of the project, everybody should discuss their plans and goals.

Building a Mitten Tree

A mitten tree is a good example of a small project performing a lot of good. Many poor families can't afford things such as gloves or mittens for their children. A mitten tree collects gloves and mittens from people who have outgrown them or have extra pairs. Contact an organization that helps families in your community. Tell them you would like to organize a mitten tree. Then your group can ask for donations from local citizens, businesses, and community groups.

RECRUITING VOLUNTEERS

Once you start volunteering, it's easy to see how much fun it can be. But how do you get others to join you? First, you have to know your school or campus. What are the best ways of getting someone's attention? Maybe a display table in the cafeteria would be a good start. Have a sign-up sheet for people who are interested. Ask them who they are,

*Others can participate when information
becomes available through flyers.*

what they'd like to do, and what they are
good at doing.

Once you have a list of people, see if they
have any common interests. Try to group
people together who like to do the same
things. Keep in mind that everyone has different talents. Maybe someone knows how to
write a press release. Someone else might be
good at designing flyers. Everyone can offer
something special. Get to know each volunteer so that you can best use his or her talents.

WRITING A MISSION STATEMENT

When it comes time to speak with adults about your group, they will want to know what kind of group you are running. They will want to know your goals and how you hope to achieve them. It will help you to answer their questions if your service-learning group has a written document stating its goals and plans. This is called a mission statement.

Toys for the Sick

Let's say your group is called "Toys for the Sick." You plan to collect toys to give to hospitalized children during the holidays. Your mission statement could read something like this:

"Toys for the Sick is a volunteer service group. We believe that children in hospitals deserve to celebrate the holidays just as much as other children do. We volunteers will use our free time to collect toy donations from students' families, from store owners, and from public officials. Toys for the Sick will deliver these donated toys to hospitals. Hospital officials will distribute the toys to sick children during the holidays."

GETTING THE OKAY

When you get a group together, you need to make sure everybody has permission to participate. You will need to talk to the following people:

Parents

Parents will want to know where their children will be and how much time your project will require. Will your group meet after school or on the weekends? Will it take away too much

You can use a computer to write a mission statement for your group.

time from their son's or daughter's home-work? Write up a permission slip that explains the project and time commitment. Get each group member to get his or her parent's or guardian's signature.

Teacher/Principal

Make sure you have permission to work on your project in school if you need to. Will you need to meet with students during study hall or after school? You'll need permission to use a room. Will you need an overhead projector to make a presentation? You'll need to get permission to use any equipment that you need. Will you put up signs on school walls to advertise an event? A school official probably will need to approve any signs you put up.

Property Owners

Will your group activity require you to use someone else's property? For example, if you are holding a car wash to raise money for

Ask for permission to work on your project in school.

your group, you will need a parking lot in which to hold it. You will need to find an available lot and then find out who owns it.

PROMOTING YOUR PROJECT

The more people that know about your project, the better. You can get your message out with such materials as flyers, press releases, and public service announcements.

Students can make signs to advertise their project.

Flyers

Flyers are a cheap way to help you get people to join your project. Your flyer should be eye-catching and easy to read. It should have a headline. Underneath the headline, the flyer should describe your project. It should explain where and when it is going to happen. And it should describe your group.

Press Release

You will want to raise awareness in your community about your service-learning project. Write a press release to send to local newspapers, radio stations, and TV stations. Write a headline and briefly describe your project. Answer the "five Ws" (who, what, where, when, and why). Be sure to include a phone number or e-mail address where someone can contact your group for more information.

Public Service Announcement (PSA)

Every radio station or TV channel sets aside free time for announcements from the public. They are called public service announcements (PSAs). Contact your local radio station or cable channel for advice about how to submit a PSA. Your PSA should be a brief advertisement to be read on the air. It should give the basic information about your group or program, including contact information. It should be between 10 and 30 seconds long.

Recycling is a good fundraising project.

FUNDING YOUR PROJECT

Your service-learning group will need at least a small amount of money. Even if your only expense goes toward publicity, you will need to pay for the paper and ink to make your flyers, press releases, and PSAs. You also may need money for supplies.

There are many ways to raise money for your group. Some private organizations offer help for service-learning programs. Other grants (money from special funds) are available through the government. Your teacher can help you with applying for those grants.

You also can raise money through the following activities:

- recycling cans, bottles, or newspapers
- cutting lawns
- shoveling snow from driveways
- holding a car wash
- holding a bake sale

EVALUATING YOUR PROJECT

What makes service learning so special is that it's beneficial to everyone involved. Both the volunteers and the people who are helped in the project gain something. The volunteers are not only doing the work. They are learning. That's why it's important to talk about what you've done. Thinking and talking about what you've experienced is called reflection. You evaluate your efforts.

Not all of your projects will be totally successful. After you've finished with your first project, sit down together as a group and talk about it. Go over everything you did. Did you

Service-learning projects with kids can be fun!

achieve the goal? Which parts of your program worked well? Which could have worked better? What can your group do to run future projects more smoothly?

Each person in the group should examine his or her efforts. What did each of you bring to the project? Which activities did you find to be difficult? Remember: One goal of service learning is to learn more about yourself. By identifying areas in which you can improve as a volunteer, you can help yourself grow as a person.

SHARING YOUR EXPERIENCE

Make sure to share your experience with others in your volunteer group. Share your experience with people who weren't part of your group, too. When you describe your experience to others, you tell them how well the project worked for the people it was meant to help. Also, you tell new people how the project helped you. Maybe next time they will join.

One teacher took a student along on a Habitat for Humanity house-building project. The next day, he was surprised to hear the student talking to other kids about all of the work he did. The next day a few more students asked the teacher if they could help too. The teacher had the first student volunteer show the new students what to do.

> **FAST FACT**
>
> *Studies have shown that students who are involved in service-learning programs get higher grades in school. They also feel more confident.*

Sharing what you've done can take many forms. You can write an article for the school paper, make a video, or even design a Web site for your project.

SHAPING YOUR FUTURE

Service learning may not interest everyone. However, everyone can participate if they so choose. The benefits of volunteering are many and great. You'll learn new skills and learn more about yourself. You'll become a better friend, parent, and citizen.

When President Bill Clinton signed the National and Community Service Trust Act, he said that he hoped that service would be honored and rewarded. The president viewed it as an investment in the future. For service-learners, the future is what they make it.

President Clinton speaks to students about service learning.

autism a mental disorder that makes a person unable to interact with others

community service a service performed by individuals for the benefit of others

corporation a group of people who bond together for business purposes

evaluate to think about the good and bad points of something

extracurricular an activity outside of class

grant money from a special fund

investment something used to create benefits for the future

mission statement a brief written document that describes a group's ideas and goals

property land or possessions that someone owns

public service announcement (PSAs) statements that are delivered for free on the radio or on television

publicity materials used to make people know about something

recycle to reprocess things, such as bottles, so that they can be used again

resumé a list of personal work experience

rural having to do with farming, agriculture, and life in country areas

scholarship a gift of money to help a student continue his or her studies

service learning organized volunteer projects in which students learn and grow through active participation

suburb a residential district on the outskirts of a city

volunteer unpaid

Books

Forte, Imogene. *A–Z Community and Service Learning*. Nashville, TN: Incentive Publications, Inc., 1997.

Goodman, Alan. *Nickelodeon's The Big Help Book: 365 Ways You Can Make a Difference by Volunteering*. New York: Pocket Books, 1994.

Lewis, Barbara. *The Kid's Guide to Service Projects*. Minneapolis, MN: Free Spirit Publishing, Inc., 1995.

Perry, Susan. *Catch the Spirit: Teen Volunteers Tell How They Made a Difference*. Danbury, CT: Franklin Watts, 2000.

ORGANIZATIONS

Boys and Girls Clubs of America
1230 West Peachtree Street, NW
Atlanta, GA 30309
Web site: *www.bgca.org*
This site provides information about past and
present programs.

**Corporation for National Service: Learn &
Serve America!**
1201 New York Avenue, NW
Washington, D.C. 20525
Web site: *www.cns.gov/learn/index.html*
This site includes the latest news and press
releases about service learning.

National Youth Leadership Council
1910 West County Road B
Roseville, MN 55113
Web site: *www.nylc.com*
Visit the NYLC site to learn more about
programs such as Youth Salutes, Win With
Wellness, and Town Meeting on Tomorrow.

Volunteering & Service Learning
110 Noyes Hall
Columbia, MO 65211
Web site:
www.missouri.edu/~cppcwww/vsl.shtml
This site provides information on the benefits of volunteering and service learning.

Youth Service America
1101 15th Street, NW, Suite 200
Washington, D.C. 20005
Web site: *www.servenet.org*
This site helps you find service opportunities in your area. It offers advice to volunteers under age eighteen.

INDEX

About the Author

Michael A. Black has long been interested in the fields of education and working with young people. He holds a Bachelor of Arts degree in English, and has worked extensively with troubled teenagers, both as a teacher and as a police officer. He feels that service learning is an important way to help young people prepare for the future.